For my beautiful daughters Lucy and Sophie, and for our Afghan friends, who have given us an insight into a different life, and who inspire us with their courage and determination – Liz Lofthouse

Kane/Miller Book Publishers, Inc.
First American Edition 2007
by Kane/Miller Book Publishers, Inc.
La Jolla, California

Text copyright © Liz Lofthouse, 2007,
Illustration copyright © Robert Ingpen, 2007
First published by Penguin Group (Australia), 2007

Library of Congress Control Number: 2007921055
Printed and bound in China
1 2 3 4 5 6 7 8 9 10

ISBN: 978-1-933605-52-4

Ziba Came on a Boat

Written by Liz Lofthouse
Illustrated by Robert Ingpen

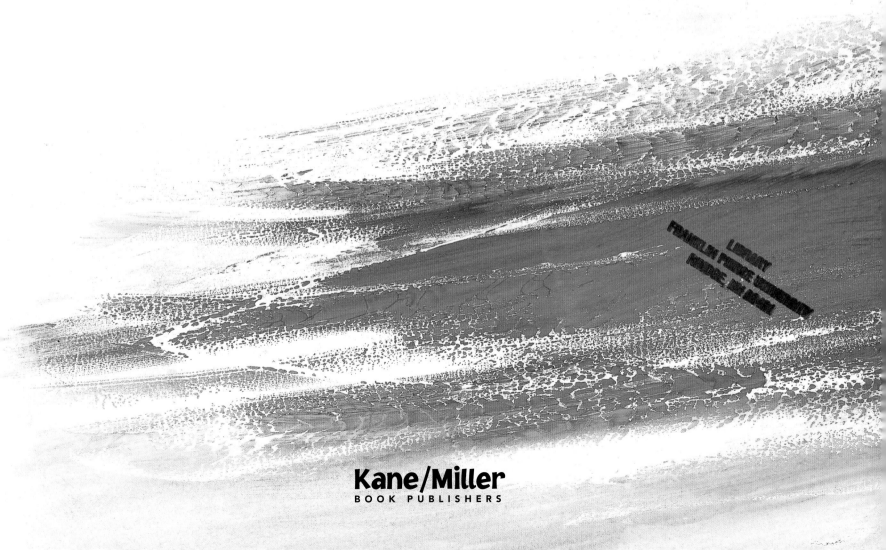

Kane/Miller
BOOK PUBLISHERS

Ziba came on a boat. A soggy old fishing boat that creaked and moaned as it rose and fell, rose and fell, across an endless sea...

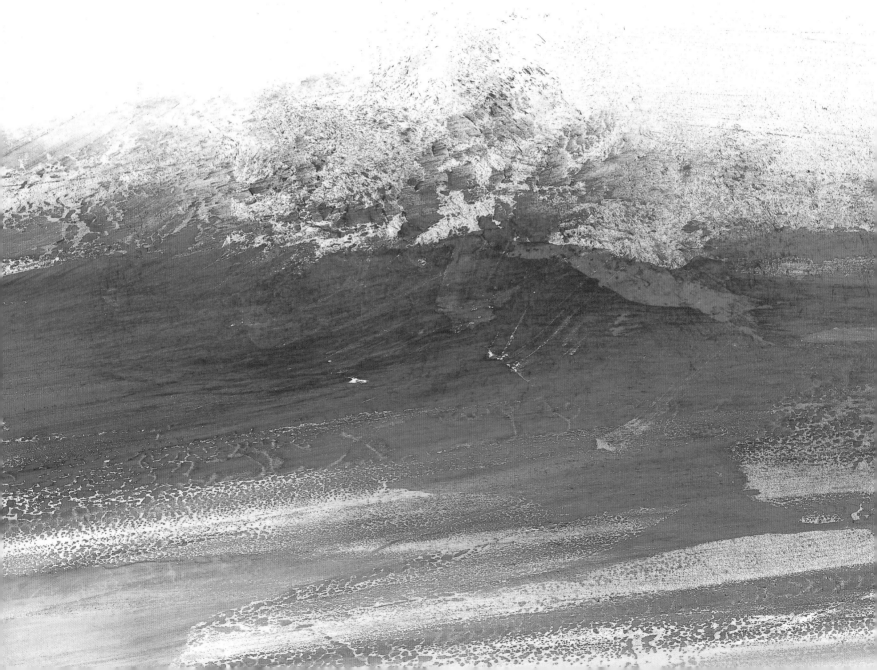

Thoughts of home washed over Ziba like the surge of the sea washing over the deck.

She heard the laughter of children and the gentle sound of sheep grazing on the hillside.

She felt the cool mountain air on her cheeks as she ran with her cousins down the rocky slope to collect water from the mountain stream.

They laughed as they splashed each other with icy water, and carried the heavy clay pots to the warmth of the mud-brick house.

Ziba smelled the rich spices of
the evening meal.

She helped her aunties prepare
the flatbread cooked in the tandur,
and tasted the cool, smooth texture
of the goat's milk yogurt her
mother made.

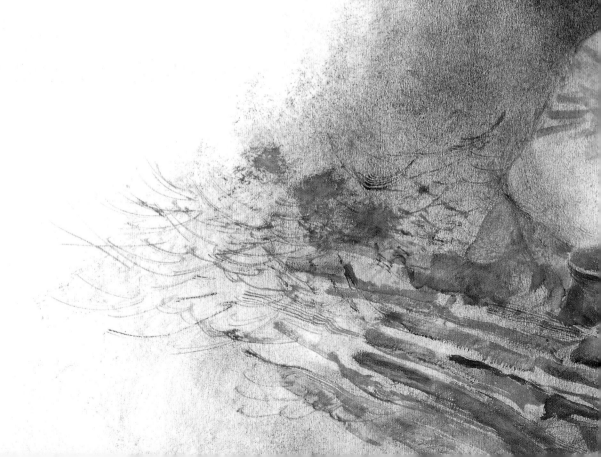

She saw her mother sitting at the wooden
loom, weaving colored wool to make a rug.

Up and down went the wool, in and out,
like the boat weaving through the murky sea.

As the boat drifted through the night,
Ziba's thoughts drifted, too.

In her mind, she sat with her father,
playing with the doll he had given her.

He told her stories and poems of long ago.
She felt the strength of his arms and
she gazed into his peaceful face.

A cool wind blew across the swirling sea.

Ziba remembered the cold winter nights
at home.

Winter had lasted so much longer that year, and the shadow cast by the mountains to the east seemed to creep closer than ever before. The darkness spread, seeping into the quiet corners of the peaceful village.

No longer able to attend school, Ziba hid from the world behind the thick earthen walls of her home.

The sea roared and thrashed
at the boat like an angry beast.
The waves became fierce, and Ziba's
thoughts grew fearful and sad.

Gunfire echoed through the village. Angry voices surrounded her. Clutching her mother's hand, Ziba ran on and on through the night, far away from the madness until there was only darkness and quiet.

Ziba shivered, and huddled closer to her mother in the crowded hull. Her mother's eyes were full of hope and her lullaby sweet as honey.

Ziba drifted into sleep.

Her dream was warm and cozy.
Smiling faces welcomed her to
a new land. Here she could live
without fear. Here she would
be free to learn and laugh,
and dance again.

"*Azadi,*" her mother whispered. "Freedom."

And the boat rose and fell, rose and fell,
across an endless sea…